Joyce
Marx
Defoe Abbott Hardy Machiavelli Montaigne Chesterton Cooper Emerson Austen
Melville Haggard Hugo
Stoker Carroll Christie Haggard Eliot Grimm
Wilde Maupassant Byron Molière
Engels Schiller
Garnett Fitzgerald Hawthorne Smith Kafka
Goethe Einstein Dostoyevsky Hall
Cotton Kipling Doyle Willis
Baum Henry Nietzsche
Leslie Dumas Flaubert Turgenev Balzac
Stockton Vatsyayana Crane
Burroughs Verne
Curtis Tocqueville Gogol Vinci
Homer Widger Tolstoy Whitman Busch
Darwin Thoreau Twain Plato Scott
Potter Freud Zola Lawrence Harte
Kant Jowett Stevenson Dickens Hesse
Andersen Burton
London Descartes Cervantes
Poe Aristotle Wells Voltaire
Hale James Hastings Cooke
Bunner Shakespeare Irving
Richter Chambers
Doré Dante Chekhov da Shaw Benedict Alcott
Swift Wodehouse Pushkin
Newton

AF303646

tredition®

tredition was established in 2006 by Sandra Latusseck and Soenke Schulz. Based in Hamburg, Germany, tredition offers publishing solutions to authors and publishing houses, combined with world-wide distribution of printed and digital book content. tredition is uniquely positioned to enable authors and publishing houses to create books on their own terms and without conventional manu-facturing risks.

For more information please visit: www.tredition.com

TREDITION CLASSICS

This book is part of the TREDITION CLASSICS series. The creators of this series are united by passion for literature and driven by the intention of making all public domain books available in printed format again - worldwide. Most TREDITION CLASSICS titles have been out of print and off the bookstore shelves for decades. At tredition we believe that a great book never goes out of style and that its value is eternal. Several mostly non-profit literature projects provide content to tredition. To support their good work, tredition donates a portion of the proceeds from each sold copy. As a reader of a TREDITION CLASSICS book, you support our mission to save many of the amazing works of world literature from oblivion. See all available books at www.tredition.com.

Project Gutenberg

The content for this book has been graciously provided by Project Gutenberg. Project Gutenberg is a non-profit organization founded by Michael Hart in 1971 at the University of Illinois. The mission of Project Gutenberg is simple: To encourage the creation and distribu-tion of eBooks. Project Gutenberg is the first and largest collection of public domain eBooks.

Sprays of Shamrock

Clinton Scollard

Imprint

This book is part of TREDITION CLASSICS

Author: Clinton Scollard
Cover design: Buchgut, Berlin – Germany

Publisher: tredition GmbH, Hamburg - Germany
ISBN: 978-3-8472-1602-5

www.tredition.com
www.tredition.de

Copyright:
The content of this book is sourced from the public domain.

The intention of the TREDITION CLASSICS series is to make world literature in the public domain available in printed format. Literary enthusiasts and organizations, such as Project Gutenberg, worldwide have scanned and digitally edited the original texts. tredition has subsequently formatted and redesigned the content into a modern reading layout. Therefore, we cannot guarantee the exact reproduction of the original format of a particular historic edition. Please also note that no modifications have been made to the spelling, therefore it may differ from the orthography used today.

[p iii]

SPRAYS OF SHAMROCK

BY CLINTON SCOLLARD

PORTLAND MAINE
THE MOSHER PRESS
MDCCCCXIV

[p 1]
SPRAYS OF SHAMROCK

[p 2]

Just a few songs of her,
Not of the wrongs of her
Many and bitter and long though they be, –
Songs of the hills of her,
Songs of the rills of her,
Ireland, set like a gem in the sea!

Just a few songs of her,
Not of the thongs of her,
She that is bound, and yet fain would be free, –
Songs of the gleams of her,
Glamours and dreams of her,
Ireland, girt by the arms of the sea!

[p 3]

MUCKROSS

A t night there came unto MacCarthy
More
A hooded vision with a voice that said,
"Go thou straightway and raise a house to God
Upon the spot where stands the Rock of Song!"
So with the golden lifting of the dawn
Upsprang the chieftain and loud called his kerns,
And bade them seek the Rock. For many a day
They roved the sweeping meads and fens and fells
In fruitless search, and ever forth again
Relentlessly he drove them from his hold
Beside the dimpling waters of Lough Leane.
"The Rock!" he cried, "find ye the Rock of Song!"
And still they found it not. Then the gaunt chief,
His long locks hoary with the frost of years,
Girded himself, and turned his tottering steps
Abroad in the soft lengthening of the dusk
Athwart a woodland close, and saw and heard
A little maid, her pitcher held at poise,
Singing an old lament in minors clear
[p 4]
And plaintive as the twilight, words that voiced

The poignant, passionate yearning of the soul.
"A sign!" the spent man whispered low, "a sign!"
And on the spot he raised a house to God.

[p 5]
THE HILL OF MAEVE

I

This is the hill of Maeve, the queen,
A mighty bulwark of gray-green

Whereon was set, by hands unknown,
A rugged monument of stone.

The great winds mourn, and sobs the wave
Beneath the lichened cairn of Maeve.

II

From many a rocky Leitrim height
O'er Lough Gill's waters, blue and bright,

From where Benbulbin fronts the foam,
And sees the Sligo ships put home,

Maeve's hill is like a pharos flame,
As is eternally her name!

III

'Neath azure tides of morning air
Ripple the waves of Ballysadare

[p 6]
Under where frowning Knocknarea
Looks o'er the Rosses far to sea, —

Looks far to sea, remembering
Maeve's loveliness, a vanished thing.

IV

The cromlechs, gray with eld, below,
Recall the dreams of long ago, —

The dreams of kern and king, both slave
To beauty, and the white Queen Maeve;

And though she slumbers, deep, so deep,
Her golden memory may not sleep!

[p 7]
AT KILLYBEGS

At Killybegs above the crags
The gray gulls pipe with voices thinned,
And all the green trees are like flags
That wave and waver in the wind.

At Killybegs about the dunes
Rustle the crispy grass and whin,
And low the long tide croons and croons
As it creeps out, as it creeps in.

At Killybegs the white sails race
When the blue sea is like a floor;
Like doubt night falls with haggard face;
Sometimes the ships return no more.

The brown bee drains the cottage flowers
Of honey to their crimson dregs,
And love hath many happy hours
'Twixt birth and death at Killybegs!

[p 8]
THE CRIPPLE

I have dreams of the outer islands,
Firths and forths of the Far-Away;
I have dreams of the heathery highlands
Under the golden day.

I have dreams of a sliding river—
Shannon—under the stars and sun;
I have dreams how the oar-blades quiver,
And the silvery salmon run.

I have dreams of a blithe lad striding
Out through the streets of Limerick-town;
I have dreams of a sweet maid biding
Under a thatch of brown.

But here I lie all huddled and hidden,
(Oh, the eternity it seems!)
Brooding desolate and bed-ridden,
Living only in dreams!

AN EXILE

I can remember the plaint of the wind on the moor,
Crying at dawning, and crying at shut of the day,
And the call of the gulls that is eerie and dreary and dour,
And the sound of the surge as it breaks on the beach of the
bay.

I can remember the thatch of the cot and the byre,
And the green of the garth just under the dip of the fells,
And the low of the kine, and the settle that stood by the fire,
And the reek of the peat, and the redolent heathery smells.

And I long for it all though the roses around me are red,
And the arch of the sky overhead has bright blue for a lure,
And glad were the heart of me, glad, if my feet could but
tread
The path, as of old, that led upward and over the moor!

[p 10]
ABBEYDORNEY

Abbeydorney, Abbeydorney,
Long ago thy race was run,
Prone thou art 'mid thickets thorny,
Shrine of Kyrie Eleison!

Scarcely now a wild rose petal
The neglected cloister owns,
And the flaunting dock and nettle
Wave above the chancel stones.

Once through Kerry twilights tender
Vesper bells their anthems tolled,
And 'mid chants, in churchly splendor,
Princely abbots were enrolled.

Tall Fitz Maurice with his crozier,
O'Clonarchy of Lismore,
They are less now than the osier
Swaying by the Cashen's shore!

Only when the moon is hidden,
Only when the moor-winds rave,
Eerily arise unbidden
Ghostly transept, ghostly nave.

[p 11]
Only when the night grows denser
March the bent monks one by one,
Singing to the sway of censer,
Kyrie – Kyrie Eleison!

So, amid thy thickets thorny,
All thy state and glory seem,
Abbeydorney, Abbeydorney,
Like a dim and fleeting dream!

A SONG FOR JOYCE'S COUNTRY

O a song for Joyce's Country, where the grim wild mountains be,
And the wind wails over the moorland as the wind wails
over the sea,
Where the new moon's silver sickle sees little of grain to
reap,
And the wraith of the mist goes creeping as soft as the feet of
sleep!

O a song for Joyce's Country, and the lonely loughs that lie,
Wrapt in the cloak of silence, under the great gray sky;
For the glens that have held in keeping for more than a thou-
sand springs
The ancient Druid wonders and the secrets of the kings!

O a song for Joyce's Country, and the graves of the mightiest
men
That ever had birth in Erin! Will their like e'er come again?
Men of the thews of titans, of the strong, unwavering hand,
Who wrested a meagre guerdon from the breast of this lean
land!

O a song for Joyce's Country, since it haunts one like a dream
That comes in the dusk ere dawning, ere the first bright sun-
rise beam;
A dream of dolor and vastness, of clouds that are swept and
swirled
O'er the desolate wastes and waters of a joy-forsaken world!

[p 14]
BALLAD OF PROTESTANT'S LEAP

It was Sir Frederick Hamilton's men
Were hungry for the fray,
And it was a son of the bog and fen
Would guide them on their way.

By the good book an oath he took,
This glib and open guide,
And so it was over bent and brook
They needs must up and ride.

They rode them fast, they rode them far,
By day's last fitful flame,
Until, by the light of the evening star,
To a heathery slope they came.

Then spake the guide, with a glint of pride,
With a catch of his breath spake he,
"Ye may fall, if over the crest ye ride,
On the Irish enemy!

"When I drop my cloak by yon stunted oak,
Do ye ply the lash and spurs,
And there 'll be no one see another sun
Of the popish worshippers!"

[p 15]
He has gone to the crest by the dwarfèd tree,
He has crept on foot and hand,
And now with a wave his cloak drops he
As a sign to the waiting band.

Oh, it's ride, Sir Frederick Hamilton's men,
Ye men of ire and brawn,
And it's smile, ye son of the bog and fen,
To see them urge swift on!

Did they purge with the sword the Irish camp?
Nay, for the story saith
Through the evening dusk, through the evening damp,
They rode to a tryst with death.

It was over a cliff that was black and sheer
To the vale of fair Glencar
That they plunged with frenzied shrieks of fear
'Neath the eye of the mountain star.

Oh, it was Sir Frederick Hamilton's men
Set forth to smite and slay,
And it was a son of the bog and fen
That guided them on their way!

[p 16]
ETCHING AT NIGHT

I wandered in the streets of Galway-town,
When night had let her dusky curtains down,
And in a doorway, tall and fair and slight,
Framed by an inner beam of golden light,
Beheld a maiden of madonna face,
Pensive and sad, yet with a nameless grace,
Presage, I thought, of the unfolding years,
That hide some things that are too deep for tears!

THE SPECTRAL ROWERS

What is that shimmering line of white
Gliding under the stark midnight—
Gliding—gliding—gliding—gliding—
Where the river gleams when the moon is bright?

There is never a sound save the night bird's cry,
And the languid water lapsing by—
Lapsing—lapsing—lapsing—lapsing—
Under the arch of a leaden sky.

'T is the winding Garavogue's spectral crew,
Bound for the port of dreams-come-true—
Rowing—rowing—rowing—rowing—
With a swinging stroke that is firm and true.

Do they ever reach their bourn? may be;
Yet who can say?—not we!—not we!—
Fading—fading—fading—fading—
Ere morn comes over the hills to the sea.

'T is so with all of the visions of man,
Howe'er he strive and howe'er he plan—
Fleeting—fleeting—fleeting—fleeting—
For life, alas, is a narrow span!

[p 18]
TYRCONNELL

They crowned Tyrconnell
On the rock of Doon;
"Hail! hail!" they said,
To that anointed head,
The henchman all;
They led him to the hall;
"Hail! hail! Tyrconnell!"
How the rafters rang!
Clang! clang!
How the blades out-sprang,
Like shimmering lake-water underneath the moon!

They slew Tyrconnell
On the rock of Doon;
"Traitor!" they said,
Of that anointed head,
The henchmen all
Who haled him from the hall;
"Base, base Tyrconnell!"
How the scabbards rang! —
Clang! clang!
As the blades out-sprang,
Like shimmering lake-water underneath the moon!

[p 19]
THE WAY OF THE CROSS

Where the wild sea-mew flocks and flees,
And neither winds nor skies beguile,
Foam-set amid the Irish seas
Is rugged Skellig Michael isle.

Up its escarpments, rough and grim,
To its bleak summit rimmed with moss,
The monks of old with prayer and hymn
Hewed out the weary "Way of the Cross."

Gone are these holy toilers — gone;
They rest now in their long repose,
From the red dusk to the red dawn,
'Neath the sea-pinks and tangled rose.

But sorrow bides with us and ill,
And stress and sacrifice and loss,
And we must strive to meet them still
Climbing the weary "Way of the Cross."

[p 20]
THE ISLE OF DOOM

Out of the mist off Galway shore,
Out of the morning mist,
Rose the island of Hy Brasail
With its crags of amethyst;

Crags of purple and amethyst,
And meads of gleaming green,
Rose the island of Hy Brasail
With a shimmer of sea between.

And what shall come to Galway shore,
What shadow of doom prevail,
With this fading dream of the mists of morn,
This island of Hy Brasail?

[p 21]
DESMOND

By the "Church of the Name" lies Desmond,
The body of Desmond lies,
And the wind of the east cries "Desmond,"
And "Desmond" the west wind cries.

And the wind of the south calls "Desmond,"
And "Desmond" the north wind calls,
As it sweeps round the keep Ardnagreagh,
The keep of the crumbling walls.

And the dawn wind grieves for Desmond,
And "Desmond" the night wind sighs;
And where is the head of Desmond,
He of the dusk-deep eyes?

They buried the body of Desmond
Hard by the "Church of the Name,"
But they hung the head of Desmond
High o'er the Gate of Shame.

Yet he was a brave man, Desmond,
A man of a hundred score,
So all the winds of the upper air,
They mourn for him evermore.

[p 22]
THE LITTLE CREEK COONANA

Oh, the little creek Coonana,
How clear it runs and cold
Where "Conn of the hundred battles"
Fought in the days of old!

Only the long wind dirges,
Only the long wind cries,
Where the giant Knocknatubber
Mounts to the vast gray skies.

Only the wind and the surges
Moan and moan and moan,
But the little creek Coonana,
It sings in a merry tone.

Only the wind and the surges
Have aught to do with fears;
Only the wind and the surges
Tell the tale of tears.

But the little creek Coonana,
It lilteth cheerily
Where the giant Knocknatubber
Glooms on the glooming sea.

[p 23]
O'DONNELL ABOO

Out of Ulster came O'Donnell,
Black O'Donnell and his crew, —
Kelly, More, Mac Carthy, Connell,
Joined the cry — "O'Donnell Aboo!"

Woe once more, red woe for Kerry,
Blood-drops were as mountain dew
When that cry so mad, yet merry,
Rang and rang — "O'Donnell Aboo!"

Gone those sanguine days of slaughter,
Sword and matchlock, pike and brand;
Peace now o'er the ways of water,
Peace o'er all the length of land.

Yet sometimes when night is sealing
Cairn and ruined shrine from view,
Down the Kerry glens goes pealing
That wild cry — "O'Donnell Aboo!"

[p 24]
NIGHTFALL IN SLIGO

I

I heard the bells of Sligo say
The tranquil requiem of day.

I saw the fires of sunset burn
Dim in the great west's golden urn.

O'er Calvary's sharp spire afar
Clear flowered one hyacinthine star.

Then mother Night her children hid
Under her purple coverlid.

[p 25]
II

Well can I recall that eve at Sligo,
And the vacant arches of the abbey
Framing the ethereal rose of sunset!
Round about me silence and gray shadow
Peopled with the wraiths of time departed,—
Monks with back-thrown cowls who pace the cloisters
Now deep-mounded, crumbled, clad with ivy.
No more from the tower their chimes of silver
Will the bells fling o'er the town and river,
O'er the Garavogue soft-gliding seaward!
Nevermore—save in deep dreams at midnight.
Death, the immemorial lord of mortals,
He is abbot in the aisles of Sligo
Till the spheres proclaim the resurrection!

[p 26]
CARROWMORE

The gray winds call o'er Carrowmore,
Call in the white of the dawn,
And the grasses sigh o'er Carrowmore
When the purple night draws on.

The cromlechs stand on Carrowmore
As they 've stood since who can say;
And the thin wraiths flit o'er Carrowmore
Between the dusk and the day.

There 's never a hush on Carrowmore
Come autumn or come spring,
For, oh, the tongues of Carrowmore,
They are fain of whispering!

And over and over Carrowmore
'T will be ever thus, meseems, —
Like the winnow of wings o'er Carrowmore
The surge of the tide of dreams!

[p 27]
ON CARAGH LAKE

I

On Caragh lake the evening light
Is violet and amethyst,
And the dark shadows of the pines
In silence keep their twilight tryst.

And high beyond the purple groves,
The sweeping moors, the climbing fells,
The rugged Kerry mountains stand
Like grim eternal sentinels.

In dying whispers on the shore
The ripples lap, the ripples break,
And there is peace beyond all words
As night descends on Caragh lake!

II

In unexpected grooves of flight
A blundering bat swoops swiftly by;
From out a coppice drifts a bird's
Last plaintive melody.

The lake is like a mirror dim
With no disturbing breath to mar,
While o'er a lonely fell there burns
One white vespernal star.

[p 28]
RAHINANE

Wrapt in mist and washed with rain
Is the hill of Rahinane;
Compassed by the hosts of sleep
Is its keep.

Only shadows come and go;
Only wraiths flit to and fro;
And the bat, grotesque and blind,
And the wind.

Just a shard of shattered hope
On a barren Kerry slope;
Just a ruin in the rain,
Rahinane!

THE WIND OF MOURNE

The wind of Mourne comes over the hill,
Over the hill with a trill of song,
And the word of the wind sets my heart athrill, —
"Though life is brief, yet love is long!"

I seek my sweet where the roses stir,
And the stars overhead are a marching throng,
And this is the tale that I tell to her, —
"Though life is brief, yet love is long!"

[p 30]
MAN AND MAID

" I know a lad in Leitrim, I know a lad," said she,
"I know a lad in Leitrim would give his heart for me!"

"I know a maid in Mayo, I know a maid," said he,
"I know a maid in Mayo would give her heart to me!"

"Go to your maid in Mayo, go to your maid," cried she;
"Go to your maid in Mayo, for all — for all of me!"

"Go to your lad in Leitrim, go to your lad," cried he,
"Go to your lad in Leitrim, for all — for all of me!"

"And yet — and yet —" she faltered, "and yet — and yet,"
blushed she,
"That lad may stay in Leitrim! It 's here I 'd rather be!"

[p 31]
"And yet — and yet —" he echoed, "and yet — and yet —"
smiled he,
"That maid may stay in Mayo. It 's there I 'd have her be!"

'T is merry down in Kerry beside the laughing sea;
'T is merry down in Kerry when man and maid agree!

[p 32]
THE HUNTER

I crept up Benbulbin a-hunting the boar;
Mist swooped on the heather, mist swept down the shore,
And all of the tongues of the mountain, they murmured be-
hind and before.

Then out of a cleft rose a terrible cry,
And a form like a demon went ravening by,
And I fell in a quake on the moss, and I thought I should die.

I 'm no hunting man now, and I sit by the fire,
And whenever the wind keens around by thc byre,
I shiver and rock like a reed that has root in the mire.

And if you 're a young man, and sound to the core,
And a sweet maid is waiting you home at the door,
Beware how you creep up Benbulbin a-hunting the boar!

[p 33]
RAIN SONG

Oh, it 's gray rain in the valleys,
White rain where the moorland lies,
And in from the bleak sea-borders
A gust that keens and cries.

Sheep huddle in the hollows,
And the cattle seek the byre,
But I must be up and faring
Away from the warm peat fire;

I must be up and faring,
For this is the hour of tryst,
And Sheilah will be waiting
At the glen amid the mist.

Oh, what 's gray rain to lovers,
And what though white rains fall,
When blue skies shine in Sheilah's eyes
For a lad of Donegal!

[p 34]
A ROVER

Oh, I am just a rover
Among the roving men
Who loves to watch the sunlight
Upon the flowering fen;

Who fain would feel the heather
Dew-soft beneath his tread
When morning parts the cloud-wrack
Above Benbulbin's head;

Who likes to lie and linger
Until the rising moon
Shows all her midnight glories
High o'er the Lough of Cloon;

Whose feet were shaped to follow
The road's eternal lure
From stormy Stockarudden
To sunny Knockanure!

But since there 's Sheilah calling,
('T is love that 's in her call!)
Faith, I am just a rover
Who 'll rove no more at all!

QUEENS

Fair Maeve, that was queen of Beauty,
Whither, whither has she gone?
Ask the cairn that over Sligo
Lifts its stones to greet the dawn!

Deirdre, that was queen of Sorrow,
Whither, whither has she fled?
Ask the woods of Finglas Water
That once knew her lissome tread!

Queens! — they are no more than mortal;
Even they must pale and pass
Like the prismy dews of dawning
On the heather and the grass!

THE WONDERS

I dream of the ancient wonders, of the isle of Hy Brasail
That rides through the mists of Mayo, then fades like a fad-
ing sail;
I dream of the ancient wonders, but there 's one that haunts
me more,
'T is the faun-like grace of Moira upon Lough Corib's shore.

I dream of the ancient wonders, of the wells of Death and
Life,
Of the voices of the Forest that quell both hate and strife;
I dream of the ancient wonders, but greater than them all
Is the luring laugh of Moira when day 's at evenfall.

I dream of the ancient wonders, of the Cross caught up in air,
Of the swan of sweet Feale Water that was a maiden fair;
I dream of the ancient wonders, but each fades in eclipse
At the lifted arms of Moira, and Moira's lifted lips!

[p 37]
AT MONAREE

When springtime comes to Monaree I know
How the blue hyacinths blow,
And how the daffodil lights its golden glow.

These blossoms are remembrancers of those
Who lie in long repose,
Lost to our earthly scenes of joys and woes, —

The saints of other days. How fair to see
These living emblems be
Of their good deeds — with spring at Monaree!

[p 38]
HEATHER SONG

Blue weather, blue weather abroad on the moors,
And the cry of the wind that elates and allures;
Sing "hey" and sing "ho" for the heather!

The brook in the bracken, it prattles and purls,
And the lips of the rose are as red as a girl's;
Sing "hey" and sing "ho" for the heather!

And the path that leads up from the stile at the start
Is the path of my longing, the path of my heart;
Sing "hey" and sing "ho" for the heather!

For I know I shall find her, my fair heather-bell,
In the warm little dip at the crest of the fell,
And her smile, ah, the burden of love it will tell!
Sing "hey" and sing "ho" for the heather!

OFF CONNEMARA

Off the coast of Connemara,
Sailor, sailor, what 's the hail?
"Dip the sail to Saint Macdara —
Dip the sail!"
So we dipped it as we tripped it
Southward with the fluting gale.

Long ago did Saint Macdara
Pass beyond this mortal pale;
Yet to-day off Connemara
Deeds of godliness avail;
Where the good old saint said masses
Every sailor, as he passes,
Dips the sail.

POPPIES AT MONASTERAVEN

As clear on my mind are graven
As the carving upon a shield
The poppies at Monasteraven,
And the cottage in the field;

The glint of a thick thorn coppice
Greenly girdling all,
And the glow of the scarlet poppies
Under the cottage wall!

Just a fleeting vision
Caught as I hurried by,
A little scene elysian
Under the morning sky.

For some one a happy haven,
It thus to my heart appealed,
The poppies at Monasteraven,
And the cottage in the field.

THE GLEN OF CASTLEMAINE

Oh, the shadows they lie deep in the glen of Castlemaine,
Purple as the gulfs of sleep, gray as are the drifts of rain!
Here are eerie feet that creep when the moon is on the wane.

In the glen of Castlemaine there are eldritch tongues that call;
And the little leaves have words that will hold the heart in
thrall.
In the glen of Castlemaine there 's a glamour over all.

For the fays have cast their spell o'er the glen of Castlemaine;
There is brooding wonder there, but no dream of blight or
bane;
Here, if you have loved and lost, you may find your love
again!

SONG

Just the sun on a slope of heather,
The long blue wind and the open sea;
All the cares of the world in tether,
And nobody there but you and me!

That 's my wish in the golden weather;
Love, you echo the wish with me?
Come, then, ho, for the slope of heather,
The long blue wind and the open sea!

[p 43]
KILMELCHEDOR

Far removed from strife and war
Is the shrine of Kilmelchedor;
O'er one crumbling archway see
Clearly graven—*Domine!*

Master then and master still,
How we lean upon His will
Who forevermore will be
Unto all men—*Domine!*

[p 44]
AT DINGLE

At Dingle, upon sand and shingle,
Softly the ripples curve and creep;
Without the white-caps meet and mingle,
Without the breakers range and leap.

Here there is calm, here there is quiet,
And the sweet sense of long delay;
There time and tide by winds that riot
Seem from their moorings swept away.

Which will you choose from life, my masters,—
Where waves are lulled to dream at ease,
Or, in the face of grim disasters,
To sail with daring down the seas?

BACK TO KILLARNEY

Oh, it 's back to Killarney, the glow and the gleam of it,
Back to Killarney for me;
Back to Killarney, the vision and dream of it,
Back to Killarney, my own countrie!

Back to Killarney at sun or at shower-time,
Back to Killarney for me;
Back to Killarney at frost or at flower-time,
Back to Killarney, my own countrie!

Back to Killarney whose soil seems a part of me,
Back to Killarney for me;
Back to Killarney to soothe the sad heart of me,
Back to Killarney, my own countrie!

[p 46]
GLENCAR WATER

I stood by Glencar Water
When spring filled all the air,
And, oh, by Glencar Water
It 's a lovely place to fare!

The song of Glencar Water
It has such silvery frets;
And there, by Glencar Water,
Are banks of violets.

But harsh seems Glencar Water
To Norah's soft replies,
And the flowers by Glencar Water
Are naught to Norah's eyes!

FROM DERRY TO KERRY

' T wixt Derry and Kerry there 's many a mile;
They 've right men in Derry, no doubt;
But give me the Kerry man's blarneying smile,
And give me the Kerry girl's conjuring wile,
And lips, like a peach, in a pout!

And give me the sails tacking in to Tralee,
And the dip of the bluff Dingle bows,
And under Beenaman the surge of the sea,
The heathery slopes that are haunts for the bee
Where Carraghmore raises its brows!

From Derry to Kerry the leagues they are long
For a foot-weary rover to wend,
But I take the far track with a snatch of a song,
And a ready forgetting of aught that is wrong,
If Kerry 's the goal at the end!

[p 48]
A KING IN KERRY

I dreamed a dream, mavourneen, I dreamed a dream yestreen,
That I was King in Kerry, and you were Galway's Queen.

I roused and ranged about me three score of burnished
spears,
And rode across the moorland, the north wind round my
ears.

It bore me buoyant tidings, — your beauty and your grace, —
And, as I galloped forward, I yearned upon your face.

We fared by Abbeydorney, Listowel and Lixnaw,
Where all my word was wisdom, and all my look was law.

We never paused to bivouac; we never paused to sleep
Where murmurous Feale Water ran shallow or ran deep.

[p 49]
We swam the swirl of Shannon; we hurled back to his lair
The blustering O'Brien who ruled the kerns of Claire.

Then, mire and foam-bespattered, about the dusk of day
We came where Galway's turrets loomed over Galway's bay.

The silence throbbed with trumpets, tumultuous, elate,
And you, a flower of wonder, bloomed in the castle gate.

You made the flush of sunset seem but a pallid thing;
Your voice had all the rapture that trembles through the
spring.

Within your eyes the love-light was glory after drouth;
All summer's hoarded honey was one kiss from your mouth.

Deirdre, whose tragic beauty the great Cuchullin knew,
And Maeve, the long lamented, sooth, what were they to
you!

[p 50]
In through the rush-strewn hallway you led us to the feast;
And when the wine was drunken there stood the stolèd
priest.

He oped the holy bride-book; he read the marriage rite;
And then — and then — mavourneen, it was our wedding
night!

Would I might dream it over, the dream I dreamed yestreen,
That I was King in Kerry, and you were Galway's Queen!

[p 51]
A KERRY LAD

There 's a Kerry lad a-wandering across the dipping sea,
A Kerry lad a-wandering the foam,
And oh, the swelling joy of it, the joy that there will be
When that wandering Kerry lad comes home!

There 'll be glad voices calling him, glad voices in the street,
And hands to clasp the hands of the gossoon;
There 'll be soft winds a-whispering above the fields of peat,
And little birds a-carolling in tune!

The Kerry sky 'll be bluer then, for all the clouds will part,
And greener 'll be the grass above the loam,
And oh, the happy feeling in one lonely Irish heart
When that wandering Kerry lad comes home!

[p 52]
A KERRY DAY

Under the sweep of a fell the smoke-reek curls and drifts
Where a white-walled cottage stands nestling amid the
green;
Kerry skies above arched with their azure rifts
Where a glint of sun peeps through to brighten the peaceful
scene.

Cattle stand at graze, and there are the piles of peat,
And there is the swift Feale Water rimpling, dimpling away;
And there are the cocks of hay, and the smell of the hay is
sweet,
And this is the round and sum of a quiet Kerry day!

A KERRY ROAD

Snow of the blackberry bloom, purple of heather bells,
The fir and the oak tree boughs with the ivy round them
twining;
Sheen of a distant lake, brown of the dipping fells,
Racing clouds overhead, and the fitful sun a-shining!

Bracken and thorn and whin, and somewhere a cheeping
bird;
Pits of peat, and, then, a cart with its cheery load;
In from Dingle Bay the wind with its ancient word;
On and up and on — and this is a Kerry road!

[p 54]
A KERRY GARDEN

There 's a garden that slopes to the south and the sun,
A garden in Kerry I know,
Where the poppy 's a-bloom, and the red roses run
O'er the wall, and the pampas-plume's streamers seem spun
Of the floss of the moon in the dusk watches won,
And the lake is a-shimmer below.

There 's a garden that 's fair, be it day, be it night,
A garden in Kerry I know,
And never an orient dream of delight
Can match with this garden so sweet to my sight,
For here is heart's home to a wandering wight, —
It calls me wherever I go!

[p 55]
DOWN IN KERRY

Down in Kerry maids are merry,
Down in Kerry maids are fair;
Laughin' eyes an' lips o' cherry
From Feale Water to Kenmare!

Sunny weather in the heather,
Sunny weather everywhere,
Be but man an' maid together
From Feale Water to Kenmare!

Care a-sheddin', naught a-dreadin',
With just one my steps to share,
That 's the road that I 'd be treadin'
From Feale Water to Kenmare!

HOLY WELLS

At Toberaribba,
Sooth, what do you think,
'T is not holy water
They go for to drink!

At Tobernanavin,
As sure as you 're born,
There 's dancing and prancing
And juice of the corn!

At Tobernacerta,
They sport on the green;
There 's laughing and chaffing,
And lots of poteen!

At Tobernaglashy,
With moss at the brink,
There 's much holy water,
But not for to drink!

[p 57]
LOW TIDE

The sun on the reeds an' rushes,
An' the sand outstretched before,
An' the sun on the kelp an' shingle
Away off Galway shore.

An' the sun on the rocks behind me,
Bright on the gorse an' whin,
An' the sun on the slantin' dories
With their white sails tackin' in.

Oh, I 'll be gay o' the sunlight,
Glad of its glint an' grace,
If its beams will only show me
The smile on one sailor's face!

[p 58]

THE "BOHAREEN" [1]

In the kingdom they call "Kerry" there 's a "bohareen" goes
climbin'
Above the thatch o' cots at Ballymore —
A little rovin' footway — an' the goat bells keep a-chimin'
In the heather slopin' upward from the shore

For the slopes are clad with heather, noddin' heather, purple
heather,
Where the bees make honey-music in the noon;
An' if you should chance to stray there in a scrap o' sunny
weather
A warbler will be tossin' you a tune.

An' you can look to seaward through the gray-green gulf o'
wonder
An' watch the slantin' sails a-dippin' far,
An' you can mark about you how the rocks are rent asunder,
An' the heights are mountin' up to reach the star.

[p 59]
But it 's not the sea below it, nor the craggy crests above it,
Nor the bracken with the mosses soft between,
Nor the droopin' bells o' heather, nay, it 's not for these I
love it,
That wanderin', that windin' "bohareen!"

But a thought that keeps a-chimin' in my heart like tender
rhymin'
Of one who clambered upward from the shore —

Whose feet with mine kept timin' as the pair o' us went climbin'
Long ago that "bohareen" at Ballymore!

1 "Bohareen," bypath.

[p 60]
AN IRISH IDYL

As I stood amid the bracken, as I stood amid the fern,
I could hear the merry bicker, the blithe bicker of the burn.
Bees were hummin', softly hummin';
"She 's a comin'! She 's a comin'!"
With a little spurt of laughter called the brook at every turn.

"Watch her! watch her! watch her! watch her!" cried a curlew
overhead;
An' I knew that it was Norah by the trippin' of her tread;
An' a gentle wind a croonin'
In the silence of the noonin' —
"Dare you kiss her? dare you kiss her?" were the saucy
words it said.

Sure, it stirred the heart within me, did that tauntin' of the
wind,
For the selfsame heart I mentioned was a sort of darin' kind;
When she came within my reachin'
There was no pause for beseechin',
For I kissed her, an' I kissed her, an', faith, Norah didn't
mind!

[p 61]
AN IRISH LASS

My love has kissed me on the lips an' sailed beyond the sea,
An', sooth, that was a sorry day for Terrence an' for me,
An' yet I whispered him "God speed" his fortune for to win,
For there 's little gold in Ireland save that upon the whin!

Like weary feet the days drag by; the heart o' me is sad;
The keenin' o' the wind at night, it nearly drives me mad;
The cries o' children in the street, they quaver lorn an' thin,
For there 's little gold in Ireland save that upon the whin!

But when my own lad comes again, ah, colleen, 't will be
sweet;
There 'll be the peal o' weddin' bells across the fields o' peat;
Faith, I can hear him sayin' it, with his shy sort o' grin,
"There 's more gold now in Ireland than that upon the
whin!"

[p 62]
THE BRIDGE OF LUCKEEN

One day as I stood at the Bridge of Luckeen,
Above the bright water all glancin' an' green,
There strayed down the path from the top of the pass
Such a slim little, prim little, trim little lass.

"Oho!" then quoth I, and "aha!" murmured she,
With as pretty a curtsy as ever you 'd see;
"Won't you pause?" I inquired; "I don't mind," said her
mien,
So we looked, side by side, from the Bridge of Luckeen.

How the minutes flew by, an' the stream how it flowed,
While never a soul came along by the road;
An' I thought her eyes sweeter than Maeve ever knew,
An' she deemed me far bolder than Brian Boru!

There 's a priest that ties knots, so the knowin' ones say,
In a neat little church in the town of Glenbeigh;
[p 63]
If he 'll tie just one more, I 'll be thinkin', I ween,
If there 's luck anywhere, there is luck at Luckeen!

[p 64]
DONEGAL

We made Donegal in the teeth of gray weather,
We made Donegal with the wind blowing free,
And the spindrift at toss like a snowy gull's feather
Where the highlands lean down to the lips of the sea.

We left Donegal in the azure blue weather,
We left Donegal with a soft breeze a-lee,
With bees in the broom and the sun on the heather,
And scarcely a ripple astir on the sea.

But give me to come in the teeth of gray weather,
Oh, give me to come with the wind blowing free,
And love's arms to clasp in their welcoming tether
A wanderer worn with the toils of the sea!

For 't is sorrow to go in the azure blue weather,
'T is sorrow to go with a soft breeze a-lee,
[p 65]
Leaving love's yearning arms where one fain would find
tether,
Watching dear Donegal sinking down in the sea!

[p 66]
AN IRISH SONG

Over me lifts the peat-reek
That parts and drifts and veers,
And the wind's uneasy moaning
Is loud about mine ears.

The waves upon the shingle
They murmur drearily,
And the streamers of the fog-wraith
Drive in from the open sea.

The mist hangs over the passes,
The mist hangs over the moors,
And the eerie cry of the curlew
It quavers and endures.

And it all is lonely, lonely,
And there 's sorrow on every face,
But the heart of me needs must love it,
For the land is mine own place!

[p 67]
TWO HUNDRED AND FIFTY COPIES OF THIS BOOK PRINTED
ON VAN GELDER HAND-MADE PAPER AND THE TYPE DIS-